POPCORN

Story by Rowena   Illustrated by Angela Archer

POPCORN

by

Rowena Womack

Published by
WEE CREEK PRESS
www.weecreekpress.com
An Imprint of
WHISKEY CREEK PRESS
PO Box 51052
Casper, WY 82605-1052
www.whiskeycreekpress.com

Copyright 2013 by Rowena Womack

Ebook ISBN: 978-1-61160-901-1
Print ISBN: 978-1-61160-595-2

Illustrator: Angela Archer
Editor: Rowena Womack
Interior Design: Jim Brown
Printed in the United States of America

With praise and thanksgiving, and with a humble heart, this book is dedicated to the glory of God the Father, Son, and Holy Spirit, who has showered me with innumerable blessings, among which are my six children, Steven, Diane, Robert, Thomas, Jonathan and Jerald, all of whom like popcorn.

I really like popcorn.
It's the best thing to eat.
It's much better by far,
Than candy, for a treat.

So this particular evening
It came to my mind.
I'd have some popcorn
To help me unwind.

The amount of kernels in the pan
Didn't look like half enough.
For my mouth was really watering
At the thought of that good stuff.

So I added another cup or two
To the oil that was hot;
Put a lid on the pan, and waited
for it to pop.

When I heard the popping begin
I was filled with glee,
For soon I'd have a pan full
Of popcorn for me.
The popping got louder
And to my surprise
The lid came off the pan
Before my startled eyes.

The popcorn was exploding.
It was in the air.
It was all over the stove.
It was everywhere.
I tried to catch it
By opening the oven door.
But it filled the oven
Then fell to the floor.

I hurried to the closet
To fetch the broom,
And when I returned,
It had spread to the next room.
I stared in disbelief.
I became quite forlorn,
For my house quickly became
Filled with popcorn.

What could I do?
I could not guess
How I would be able
To clean up this mess.
Then a thought came to me
And within a minute.
I was happy my house
Had so much popcorn in it.

For now I could have popcorn
Morning, noon, and night!
What a wonderful happening!
What a tasty delight!
I had it for breakfast,
For dinner and lunch
And in between meals
On that popcorn I'd munch.

And before I knew it,
I awoke one day
To find I had eaten
All of that popcorn away.
If you like popcorn
And it comes to mind
That you'll have yourself some
To help you unwind,

And if you think you're hungry
For a lot of that good stuff,
Remember, a small amount of
Kernels in the pan
Is probably quite enough!

About the Author

Rowena Womack was born during the Great Depression with tuberculosis and re-contracted the disease at the age of twelve. She spent three years in isolation at the Irene Byron sanatorium in Ft. Wayne, Indiana, one of the youngest patients ever treated for pulmonary tuberculosis with pneumathorax treatment. Despite these early health setbacks, Rowena maintained a thankful spirit and determination to succeed, graduating in the top ten per cent of her high school class, excelling in speech, debate, writing, music and mathematics. For fourteen years she was a single mother with five sons and a daughter, and today she counts many grandchildren and great grandchildren in the family fold. A cancer survivor, she remains the thankful spirit, guided by her Christian faith. She finds joy in the smallest details of life too, much as a child might do. Rowena is the author of the children's books POPCORN and YELLOWSTONE MOOSE, and the scheduled 2014 releases GOOFUSUS ETC and BALLS.

About the Illustrator

Angela Archer is a biologist by training but an artist at heart. She uses her love of animals and the natural world around her to inspire her art. While traditional media still has a place in her tool kit, these days most of her projects are done digitally. These illustrations were created with Photoshop and Sketchbook Pro. She uses a Wacom tablet and a Mac. She makes her home in rural Minnesota with her daughter and husband.

CPSIA information can be obtained
at www.ICGtesting.com
Printed in the USA
LVXC02n0903240314
378658LV00002B/3